Alex and T-Bone, her dog, were almost asleep when a sudden scratching noise made her sit upright in bed. "T-Bone! Wake up! What if there's a burglar in here?" The dog slowly opened one eye and closed it again.

SCRATCH! SCRATCH! SCRAPE! went the noise again. It sounded as if it were coming from inside her closet.

T-Bone was wide awake now. He barked and leaped from the bed.

"Mom! Dad!" Alex hollered. "Help! There's something horrible up here!"

The ALEX Series
by Nancy Simpson Levene

- Shoelaces and Brussels Sprouts
- French Fry Forgiveness
- Hot Chocolate Friendship
- Peanut Butter and Jelly Secrets
- Mint Cookie Miracles
- Cherry Cola Champions
- The Salty Scarecrow Solution
- Peach Pit Popularity
- T-Bone Trouble
- Grapefruit Basket Upset
- Apple Turnover Treasure
- Crocodile Meatloaf

The
Salty Scarecrow
Solution

Nancy Simpson Levene

Chariot Books™

Chariot Books™ is an imprint of
David C. Cook Publishing Co.
David C. Cook Publishing Co., Elgin, Illinois 60120
David C. Cook Publishing Co., Weston, Ontario
Nova Distribution Ltd., Newton Abbot, England

THE SALTY SCARECROW SOLUTION
© 1989 by Nancy Simpson Levene for text and GraphCom
Corporation for interior illustrations

Cover design by Bill Paetzold
Cover illustration by Neal Hughes

First Printing, 1989
Printed in the United States of America
98 97 96 95 94 9 8 7 6

Library of Congress Cataloging-in-Publication Data
Levene, Nancy S., 1949-
The salty scarecrow solution / Nancy Simpson Levene;
illustrated by Susan Morris.
p.   cm.
Summary: A young girl's religious beliefs help her to make
the right decision when she competes for the scarecrow role
in the school play.
ISBN 1-55513-523-4
[1. Plays—Fiction. 2. Schools—Fiction. 3. Christian
life—Fiction.] I. Morris, Susan, ill. II. Title.
PZ7.L5724Sal 1989
[Fic]—dc19   89-31274
                                                      CIP
                                                      AC

To our Father God
who makes the salt
and passes the shakers to His children
and
To Ann Schmidt
who generously sprinkles her salt,
richly flavoring the lives of many
(especially mine).

And let us not get tired of doing what is right, for after a while we will reap a harvest of blessing. . . .

Galatians 6:9
The Living Bible

ACKNOWLEDGMENTS

Thank you, Ann and Lindsay, for our wonderful but tough choir year, and thank you, Cara, for living through these experiences for Alex and her readers in such a godly manner.

CONTENTS

CHAPTER 1

Trouble with Tyler

"I know you will do great, Alex," Janie encouraged her friend.

"Do you really think so?" Alex asked nervously. She pushed the straw hat down firmly on her head and stuffed the prickly straw into the tops of her boots.

Janie tied the bandana around Alex's neck and adjusted the rope belt.

"You look like a perfect scarecrow, Alex," she said. "Don't worry. Mrs. Parrott is sure to pick you for the part."

Alex looked anxiously over at Mrs. Parrott. The music teacher sat on a chair in the middle of the gymnasium floor and called out directions to the children on the stage in front of her.

The children were trying out for parts in the

third and fourth grade play. This year it was to be a musical—*The Wizard of Oz.*

At the moment, the stage was full of girls trying out for the part of Dorothy. They wore gingham dresses and shiny shoes. Alex frowned. She would much rather be a sloppy scarecrow.

All at once, Mrs. Parrott clicked a button on her recorder. The song "Over the Rainbow" stopped. "Very good, very good," called Mrs. Parrott to the girls on stage. "You all did just fine." The teacher checked her watch. "We have time for one more group. Scarecrows! Line up on the stage, please."

Alex and three other chileren ran to the stage. They were all dressed in baggy pants or overalls and big flannel shirts. Alex smiled to see that she was the only scarecrow to have real straw peeking out of the sleeves of her shirt and the tops of her boots. She had grabbed a handful of straw out of T-Bone's doghouse that morning.

Just as Mrs. Parrott was about to start the music, another scarecrow ran on stage. Alex gasped. It was Tyler Forbes, and he wore the best scarecrow costume of all. His shirt was baggy and faded to just the right color of green. It matched the patches on his brown pants. But the best, the very best, part of Tyler's costume was the hat—a pointed, but soft and floppy, just perfect-for-a-scarecrow hat.

"Tyler Forbes, where did you get that hat?" Mrs. Parrott asked.

"My mom made it," Tyler answered smugly.

"You mean your mom made you a costume just for the tryouts?" Alex exclaimed.

"Of course," Tyler answered with a scowl. "My mom wants me to get the part."

"Well, my mom wants me to get the part, too," Alex replied. "But she would wait until I got it before making a costume."

Tyler shook his head. "Too bad," he told her.

Mrs. Parrott clapped her hands for silence. One by one, the five scarecrows sang and danced their solos. Alex was the last. As she watched the first three children, her confidence grew. She knew she could do better. But Alex's heart sank when Tyler began. He was really good. Was he better than she? Maybe she should do that flip at the end of her act after all. She had decided that it was too risky—she might flip off the stage. But, on second thought, it just might be the spectacular touch that she needed to help her beat Tyler.

"Very good, Tyler," Mrs. Parrott called as the music ended. "Alex, it's your turn."

Alex glanced at Janie for support. Her friend waved in encouragement. Alex took a deep breath. The music started. Soon, her nervousness left and Alex sang loudly, sliding and jerking around the stage in true scarecrow fashion. Even the flip at the end turned out well. Alex landed on her feet, well away from the edge of the stage.

Alex's friends clapped long and loud at the end of her performance. Mrs. Parrott smiled and said, "Very good, Alex."

"You were great, Alex," Janie shouted.

"Yeah, I'm sure you'll get the part," added Julie, another friend.

"I don't know," replied Alex. "Tyler Forbes was pretty good, too."

"But not as good as you," Janie quickly

said. "He didn't fall on the ground as many times as you did, and he didn't do a flip, either!"

"Did you know his mom made him that costume for the tryouts?" Alex said. "Whoever heard of such a thing?"

Alex and her friends started to leave the gym to go back to their classroom, but Alex stopped suddenly and caught her breath. Tyler stood before her, blocking her path. He glared at her angrily, then turned and walked away.

"What's his problem?" Janie asked.

"I'm sure he's mad because I'm trying out for the same part he is," said Alex.

"He's a spoiled brat," Julie declared.

"He's an only child who gets everything he wants," observed Janie.

"Yeah, including a scarecrow costume," Alex grumbled.

When they returned to the classroom, it was noisy. The children were excited about the tryouts and called loudly to one another.

"Hey, Alex!" Joshua Barton shouted. "You looked pretty flipped out on stage!" He laughed. "Flipped out! Get it?"

"That's so funny, I forgot to laugh," replied Alex. She gave Joshua a sour look.

"Oh, Alex would make an excellent scarecrow," teased another boy. "She's clumsy enough for the part!"

Alex rolled her eyes toward the ceiling, folded her arms across her chest, and did not say a word. If she could ignore those boys long enough, they would eventually stop their teasing. Fortunately, she did not have to try for very long. "Let's all settle down!" Mr. Carpenter, their teacher, called as he strode through the doorway. "Tryouts are over for today. We will now go over last night's math homework. Get out your papers, please."

Alex sighed and moaned with the rest of the class. It was hard, but somehow she managed to turn her thoughts from the tryouts to math problems.

After school, Alex waited outside for Janie. It was such a beautiful spring day that Alex could not stay one more minute inside the school building.

This was a very special day. Besides being the day of the tryouts, it was also the first day of spring softball practice. In a few minutes, she and Janie would join their team, the Tornadoes, on the softball field. Alex was the pitcher. Janie usually played right field.

Alex dragged her mitt and ball out of her backpack. She began throwing the ball high in the air and catching it with her mitt.

While circling underneath a particularly high ball, Alex was startled to feel a tap on her shoulder. Thinking it was Janie, she kept her eyes on the ball and muttered, "Wait a minute, Janie. Let me catch this ball."

"I'm not Janie!" growled a voice.

"Oh!" Alex gasped as she saw Tyler standing right beside her.

BLOP! The ball hit the ground between them and bounced up, hitting Tyler in the nose.

"OW!" Tyler yelled. He rubbed his nose angrily. Before Alex could say anything, he cried, "You're not going to be the Scarecrow! Do you hear me? I am!" Tyler picked up Alex's softball and heaved it into the air. The ball flew in a long arch above the school building and curved its way down to the roof. BONK! It hit the roof and bounced its way to the gutter where it stuck.

"Brussels sprouts!" Alex cried. "Look what you've done! My ball is stuck on the roof! Now what am I going to do, huh? That's my favorite pitching ball!"

The more she talked, the angrier Alex became. She began to yell louder and louder. Slowly at first, but then faster and faster, Tyler backed away from Alex. Finally, he turned and ran. Alex chased him out of the playground, and then returned to stare up at the school's roof.

What should she do? She could ask Mr. Carpenter for help, but he was a grown-up and grown-ups always took too long to do anything. He would try to find a long stick or use a broom to try and knock the ball down. Then whatever he used would not be long enough, so he would have to find something longer. And by that time, half of softball practice would be over.

Alex sighed. She would have to get her ball down herself, and the only way to do that was to climb up on the roof.

It didn't take Alex long to spot a way up to the roof of the school building. All she had to do was climb on top of the steel shoe scraper that stood by a doorway and pull herself up onto a window ledge that was right above it. From there, she was sure she could reach the roof and hoist herself up onto it. There was even a convenient metal pipe for support.

The first part of her plan worked easily. She reached the window ledge with no trouble. She had a few anxious moments going from the ledge to the roof, but with sheer determination and by refusing to look down, she made it.

Lying flat on the roof, Alex looked around in all directions. She wanted to make sure that no one was watching. If any teacher saw her on the roof, she would surely get into trouble.

The coast was clear. Slowly, Alex stood up and moved carefully toward the edge of the roof and the gutter that held her ball.

Even though the roof was flat, Alex felt a

kind of dizzy feeling in her stomach, especially when she looked over the edge of the roof and down to the ground below. "Just a few more steps and I'll have my ball," she told herself. Finally, she reached the gutter and stretched out her hand for the ball.

Suddenly, a door opened directly below her and loud voices shattered the stillness. Alex gasped! Janie and Mr. Carpenter walked out of the door and into Alex's view. But even worse than that, after Janie and Mr. Carpenter, came Mrs. Larson the school principal!

CHAPTER 2

Fight on Juniper Hill

Alex felt her legs stiffen and her throat tighten. From the rooftop, she stared down at the backs of the people below. What if Mr. Carpenter or Mrs. Larson turned around and saw her up here on the roof? Alex shuddered at the thought.

"I wonder where Alex is," Janie said to Mr. Carpenter. "She was supposed to meet us out here."

"Maybe she's down at the ball field already," her teacher replied.

"But she said she would wait for me right here," Janie complained.

"I don't see Alex anywhere." Mrs. Larson shaded her eyes with her hands and looked in all directions.

Up on the roof, Alex began to back away from the edge. But her foot caught on a piece of shingle and she tripped, falling heavily on her backside. The softball slipped from her hand and bounced off the roof. Alex watched in horror as the ball sailed through the air straight toward Mr. Carpenter, Janie, and Mrs. Larson.

"OUCH!" Mr. Carpenter yelled when the ball smacked his shoulder. He turned around and almost immediately spotted Alex.

"Uh, sorry," Alex called down to her teacher.

"Alex!" Janie screamed in surprise.

"Alex?" Mrs. Larson echoed. She stared at Alex for a moment in confusion and then cried, "Alexandria Brackenbury! Come down off that roof at once!"

"Okay," Alex replied and stood up.

"No! Wait!" Mrs. Larson shouted. "Sit down! We'll get someone to rescue you."

"But I don't need rescuing," Alex protested.

"Don't argue, Alex," Mr. Carpenter replied. Frowning, he turned to Mrs. Larson. "I'll go get Mr. Whitney."

Alex's heart sank. Mr. Whitney was Kingswood Elementary School's custodian. Last year, Mr. Whitney had caught Alex trying to sneak into his janitor's closet. He had not been very happy about that. Alex had tried to stay out of Mr. Whitney's way ever since.

"Uh, Mrs. Larson," Alex called in her most polite voice. "I can get down easily by holding onto that pipe and reaching the window ledge with my foot. Then, from there, I can climb down onto the shoe scraper."

"Hmmmm, well, I'm sure you can, Alex," Mrs. Larson responded. "But if you should slip and fall, it would be my fault for letting you try. I don't want to take that chance."

Alex sighed in frustration. She felt so silly sitting on top of the school building. What if that group of boys over by the swings saw her? She would never live it down!

"You mean to tell me she got all the way up on the roof?" Mr. Whitney's gravelly voice rang out as he and Mr. Carpenter strode around the corner of the school building. They carried a long ladder.

"Well, I'll be!" Mr. Whitney exclaimed when he saw Alex perched on the school roof. "How in the world did you manage to get up there? You sure are good at getting yourself into the most peculiar places!"

Alex's face turned red. Mr. Carpenter and Mrs. Larson laughed out loud.

Mr. Whitney adjusted the ladder to reach the roof. He began to climb the ladder.

Suddenly, loud voices called from the playground, "Hey! There's somebody up on the roof!"

Alex groaned as the group of boys on the playground rushed up the hill toward her.

"Okay, young lady, grab my hand and walk this way slowly." Mr. Whitney had reached the top of the ladder and was holding his hand out to her.

Alex grabbed Mr. Whitney's hand and moved toward the ladder. Her face flushed at the teasing taunts made by the boys below.

"Watch out, Alex!" they called. "Don't fall off the ladder, Alex!"

After Alex reached the ground, Mr. Carpenter sent the boys away. Then, Alex had to explain why she had been on the roof. She told her teacher, her principal, Mr. Whitney, and Janie how Tyler had thrown her softball up on the roof and how she had tried to retrieve it.

"Well, Alex," Mrs. Larson smiled after she had heard Alex's explanation. "I am glad that you were not hurt and that you got your softball off the roof."

"My softball!" Alex cried. She had forgotten all about it.

"Here it is." Janie handed Alex her ball. "I was holding it for you."

"Oh, thanks," Alex sighed in relief. She and Janie turned to run down the hill to the softball field.

"Oh, Alex," Mr. Carpenter called after her. "The next time somebody throws your softball on a roof, make sure it's a slanted roof so your ball will roll off easily!"

Alex thought for a moment and then called back to her teacher, "I'll be sure to tell that to Tyler."

Mr. Carpenter laughed.

23

After softball practice, Alex and Janie trudged up the Juniper Street hill on their way home. Alex lived in a big white house at the top of the hill. Janie lived in a big blue house right behind Alex.

Alex and Janie had spent many hours walking up and down the Juniper Street hill. They knew every curb and every bush and every house on it.

This afternoon, however, the hill was not as peaceful as usual. Loud voices screamed at the top of it. Slamming and banging sounds echoed down the hill to Alex and Janie's ears. What in the world was happening at the top of Juniper Street?

"It must be the Goblin," Alex decided. "Goblin" was Alex's nickname for her seven-year-old brother. Everyone else called him Rudy.

A sudden, high-pitched scream filled the air.

"That sounds like Jason," Janie commented. Jason lived next door to Alex and Rudy. Jason was the same age as Rudy and was his best friend.

"Come on," Alex said to Janie, "we'd better go see what's going on."

The two girls began to run up the hill, but before they had gone very far, an orange and black ball bounced down the street toward them.

"Hey! That's Rudy's soccer ball!" Alex shouted at Janie. She ran to catch it. She had no sooner done so than another ball barreled down the street. Janie caught that one. It was a basketball.

Alex and Janie stared up the hill in surprise.

Two small figures could be seen dashing in and out of the street. They seemed to be taking turns hurling objects down the street.

"Hey! Cut it out!" Alex yelled as she dodged a flying roller skate.

"Ow!" Janie shrieked when a baseball smacked her ankle.

"That does it!" Alex hollered. She charged up the street and reached the top of the hill just in time to snatch Rudy's dirt bike out of Jason's hands before Jason sent it flying down the hill.

"Jason!" Alex exclaimed. "Why would you want to throw Rudy's bike down the hill!"

"Rudy's been throwing my stuff down the hill, so I'm throwing his stuff down the hill, too!" Jason exploded.

"Well, it's your fault!" Rudy shouted at his best friend.

Alex turned to stare at her brother. She could always tell when Rudy was angry. He puffed his cheeks up like a chipmunk.

"It is not my fault!" Jason retorted. "You started it!"

"DID NOT!" screamed Rudy.

"DID TOO!" Jason hollered.

"Wait a minute! Wait a minute!" Alex tried to calm them down. She stepped in between them just as Rudy threw a punch at Jason.

"OUCH!" Alex yelled and doubled over. Rudy's punch had caught her square in the stomach.

"Sorry, Alex," Rudy apologized. "I meant to hit creepy old Jason."

"Oh, yeah?" Jason roared. "Well, how does this feel?" He dove at Rudy, knocking him to the ground. The two boys rolled over and over on the ground, each one trying to sock the other.

Janie suddenly appeared at Alex's side. Her arms were full of balls and roller skates that she had carried up the hill.

"Quick," Alex cried, "help me get Jason off of Rudy." She caught hold of one of Jason's arms.

Janie dropped the load she was carrying and reached for Jason's other arm. Together, the girls dragged him away from Rudy.

Janie held onto Jason while Alex grabbed Rudy. They had quite a time keeping the two boys away from each other.

"Now what do we do?" Janie hollered at Alex. "Ouch! Jason, stop kicking me!"

"Rudy, hold still!" Alex yelled in her brother's ear.

The two girls finally got the younger boys under control. Alex stared at Janie and laughed. Janie had wrapped one of her legs around both of Jason's legs and had criss-crossed her arms across Jason's chest, pinning his arms tightly to his sides.

"Looks like Jason's not going anywhere!" Alex giggled.

"Yeah, and neither am I," Janie replied, straining to keep her balance. "Like I said before, Alex, now what do we do?"

Alex was in the same situation. She didn't dare relax her hold on Rudy or he might wriggle free.

"Uh, let me think," Alex replied.

"Well, don't take too long," Janie warned. "Jason and I might fall over any minute."

Alex did not have to think too long because, almost immediately, a familiar blue car pulled into the driveway.

"Uh oh, Goblin, look who's here," Alex sang in her brother's ear.

She felt him stiffen as he watched their father park the car. Father did not like fighting at all. Just last week, he had let Rudy know how much he did not like fighting when Rudy had come home from school with a purple left cheek.

"Tough luck," Alex whispered. She watched Father get out of the car and walk straight toward them.

CHAPTER 3

God's Salt

Father stood between Alex and Janie. He looked curiously at the girls as they gripped Rudy and Jason tightly.

"Well, well," Father drawled. "Let me guess . . . you girls are earthlings and the boys are ferocious bat creatures from another galaxy. You're getting ready to throw them into the deactivation chamber where they will change from horrible bat creatures into gentle little butterflies."

"Dad!" Alex giggled. "That's ridiculous!"

"Well, then, are you going to tell me the real reason why you and Janie have these two darling, innocent, little boys locked in such hammerholds?"

"Darling!" Alex wrinkled her nose in disgust.

"Innocent?" Janie rolled her eyes skyward.

"I guess we could let go of them," Alex said to Janie. "Now that Dad's here, I think it's safe."

Janie looked rather doubtful. "You let go of Rudy first," she said.

Alex took her hands off her brother. Rudy dropped to the grass. He did not look at anyone or say a word.

Janie let go of Jason, who immediately ran to his house next door.

"Will someone please tell me what is going on?" Father demanded.

Alex told her father about Rudy and Jason's fight and how they had thrown each other's toys down the hill.

With a puzzled frown on his face, Father squatted down beside Rudy and peered into his son's eyes. "What's the matter between you and Jason?"

Rudy turned his head away. He did not answer.

"Watch out, Dad," Alex warned. "He's got that stubborn look on his face."

31

"Ahem," Father cleared his throat. "Would you girls mind leaving us alone for a while, please?" he asked.

"Oh, sure, Dad," Alex replied. She and Janie walked to the house. Before going inside, Alex looked back to see her father sitting on the ground beside Rudy. He looked a little funny sitting on the grass in his business suit. All the same, Alex was glad that she had a father who would do just that sort of thing.

That evening after dinner, the Brackenbury family got ready for Treasure Hunting. That was a special time they had together every Tuesday night. They would read a story in the Bible and see how that story fit into their own lives. Whatever God taught them through the story was the treasure.

Father stood in the center of the room. He wore the same sea captain's hat that he wore for every Treasure Hunt. Both Alex and Rudy laughed at Father as he pretended to sail his imaginary ship across the ocean in search of treasure.

"Okay, all you buccaneers, are you ready?

Hoist the sail! Raise that anchor! Off we go to search for treasure!'' Father held up a pretend sword and fought an imaginary duel.

"Dad, really!'' sighed Barbara. She rolled her eyes and frowned. Barbara was thirteen years old and perfect. At least she tried to make everyone think that she was perfect. It was true that she did have beautiful blonde hair and that she spent hours in the sun getting a gorgeous tan. She also wore the latest in clothes and could paint a picture so well that it was hard to tell which was the picture and which was the real thing. But was she perfect?

"No way!'' Alex said to herself. Alex tossed her own short brown hair in annoyance and tried to pinch away a stray freckle that appeared on her arm.

All of a sudden, Father turned to Alex and poked her arm with his finger. "What flavor are you?'' He pretended to taste the tip of his finger.

"Dad!'' Alex exclaimed. "I'm not any flavor!''

"You're not?'' Father widened his eyes as if

surprised. "I thought you tasted like a pepperoni pizza!"

That made Rudy howl with laughter.

"What about you, young man?" Father pretended to taste Rudy. "Uh-huh, yummmm, chocolate syrup!"

When Father turned toward Barbara, she tried to jerk her arm away, but he was too quick. He poked her arm and exclaimed, "Oh, yummy! Scrambled eggs and ketchup!"

"Oooooooh yuck!" Alex and Rudy screamed. Barbara had shocked the family that morning by dumping ketchup on her eggs.

"What about me?" Mother asked. "Aren't you going to see what flavor I am?"

"Just saving the best for last, dear," Father answered with a gallant bow. He reached out a finger and carefully "tasted" Mother.

"Yummmmmm," was all he said.

"Well, what does Mom taste like?" Rudy demanded.

"Yum! Yum!" Father licked his lips.

"Dad!" Alex hollered in frustration.

"Let's see," Father said slowly. "She tastes

absolutely wonderful . . . like sweet strawberry shortcake. Yes, that's it—strawberry shortcake with whipped cream on top."

They all laughed.

After everyone was quiet again, Father said, "It was fun pretending that we are different flavors. But did you know that as Christians we are really supposed to be flavorful?"

Alex stared at Father in surprise. "What do you mean?" she asked him. "What flavor could we be?"

"Salty!" was Father's answer. He smiled at the puzzled looks on their faces. "Jesus says in the Bible that Christians are the salt of the earth."

"But how can we be salt?" Alex exclaimed. "You sprinkle salt on food."

"That's right, Firecracker," Father agreed. "And what does the salt do to the food?"

"It makes it taste good," Alex answered, "especially french fries!"

"And popcorn," Rudy added.

"And peanuts," put in Barbara.

"Then would you all agree that salt adds

good flavor to food?" Father asked them.

"Yes," they cried.

"Well, just as salt adds flavor to food, Christians are supposed to add flavor to the world," said Father.

"But what kind of flavor can we add to the world?" Alex asked.

"Oh, we can sprinkle the people of the world with all kinds of flavors from God's salt shakers," Father answered. "Like love, peace, kindness, and forgiveness. We can flavor the world with the good things of God."

Alex and Rudy grinned at each other and pretended to dump salt on each other's heads.

"Do you remember the story of Joseph?" Father asked Rudy.

"Sure, he was the kid who got that weird coat made of millions of different colors," Rudy replied.

"Do you remember how his brothers were jealous because Joseph was his father's favorite?"

"Yeah, they put him down in a big hole and wouldn't let him up!" Rudy exclaimed.

"And they sold him as a slave," Alex added.

"Yes, they did all that to Joseph, and he was taken to Egypt as a slave. Later, he was thrown into prison for something he didn't do," said Father. "But through all of that, Joseph stayed close to the Lord. And the Lord gave Joseph a special ability. Do you remember what it was?"

"He could tell people what their dreams meant," Barbara answered.

"And Joseph told the pharaoh about his dream and the pharaoh was so glad that he got Joseph out of prison and gave him a chariot and everything!" Alex interrupted.

Father laughed. "That's right, Firecracker. The pharaoh put Joseph in charge of the whole country. Now what do you think such a powerful man like Joseph did when he finally saw his brothers again? Remember, those were the brothers that had sold him into slavery."

"He probably smushed them with his chariot!" cried Rudy.

"Rudy!" Mother exclaimed.

"Oh, yuck, Goblin." Alex covered her mouth with her hands.

"Ahem," Father cleared his throat. "I think most people would agree with Rudy. They would think that Joseph ought to get back at his brothers and hurt them. After all, they did some pretty mean things to Joseph. But instead of hurting his brothers, Joseph did the godly thing, not the worldly thing. He sprinkled his brothers with forgiveness and peace."

"And that's how we should be," added Mother. "We need to act in a godly way like Joseph. Then we are truly God's salt."

Father gave a piece of paper to each of the children. Alex looked at hers. On it was written, "Have salt in yourselves and be at peace with one another. Mark 9:50."

Rudy fiddled with his piece of paper, turning it over and over in his hands. Finally, he sighed, "I guess I better go sprinkle Jason with forgiveness."

Father, Mother, Barbara, and Alex exchanged surprised looks.

"Can I go over to Jason's right now?" Rudy asked urgently.

Father looked at his watch. "Go ahead," he

said. "We will call you inside in a few minutes."

Rudy bounced out the front door. A few seconds later, the family was surprised to hear a piercing howl just outside the living room window. The howl was followed by the squeaky sound of the outdoor water faucet. They all raced outside.

Rudy stood by the faucet, the garden hose wrapped around his legs. He was frantically moving the faucet around and around with big jerks.

"You just wait, Jason! I'll sprinkle you all right! We'll see how you like this SPRINKLE!" Rudy hollered.

In two long strides, Father was beside Rudy. He reached for the hose, but quite by accident Rudy flung the hose up and over his shoulder, hitting Father full in the face with a stream of cold water.

"AAAAAAAAHHH!" Father yelled. Stumbling around Rudy, he grabbed the faucet and yanked it hard to the right. It spun around and around easily—too easily. The

water would not shut off.

Father tried again, this time spinning the faucet to the left. The water still did not shut off. The hose flip-flopped to the right and to the left. Fountains of water spewed everywhere. "HOLD THAT HOSE STILL!" Father yelled at Rudy.

Rudy wrestled with the hose, drenching himself and Father. Alex leaped into action and tried to help Rudy steady the hose. She, too, became sopping set.

"GO TURN OFF THE WATER INSIDE!"

Father called to Mother. He pointed in the direction of the basement.

Mother hurried inside the house. Barbara followed. It wasn't long until the water suddenly stopped. The hose lay still and everything was quiet again. Everything but Rudy. He shook with sobs. Giant tears rolled down his face.

"Rudy, what happened?" Father demanded in exasperation. "I thought you were going over to Jason's house."

"I was! I did!" Rudy wailed. "I was going to apologize to Jason, but he sneaked out of the bushes and squirted me with a water pistol right in the face!"

"You mean he squirted you before you could even talk to him?" Alex exclaimed.

"Exactly!" Rudy folded his arms across his chest and stomped a foot angrily.

"So you thought you would squirt Jason back," said Father, "only with something a little bigger than a water pistol—a garden hose!"

"Yeah," Rudy admitted. "But I didn't mean to break the faucet."

"The faucet can be fixed, " Father breathed wearily. "What's more important is fixing your friendship with Jason."

"That's not going to be fixed!" cried Rudy in a loud voice. "I'm never going to talk to Jason again! NEVER!"

CHAPTER 4

Noise in the Night

"Surely Rudy will speak to Jason this morning," Mother whispered to Father and Alex at the breakfast table the next morning. "He and Jason always walk to school together."

But Rudy did not speak to Jason or walk to school with him that day or the next day or the next.

"I can't believe it," Alex said to Janie as the girls walked to school Friday morning. "It's been three whole days and Rudy and Jason haven't said one word to each other!"

But the girls quickly forgot about the younger boys as soon as they arrived at school. The classroom hummed with excited voices. Today was the day that Mr. Carpenter would announce who got what parts in *The Wizard of Oz.*

"I'm sure you'll be picked as the Scarecrow, Alex," Janie exclaimed loudly.

Tyler Forbes glared at Alex.

Mr. Carpenter began to pace back and forth in front of the class. He always paced when he had something important to tell them.

Alex sat on the edge of her chair and waited for her teacher to speak. She wanted the Scarecrow part so badly. She would just die if Tyler Forbes got it.

Mr. Carpenter called out some of the parts and the children who would play them. There were cheers and groans as he made each announcement.

"And that's all that we have decided upon so far," Mr. Carpenter ended. He picked up a book and began to teach the day's science lesson.

Alex and Janie stared at each other in alarm. Mr. Carpenter had not said a word about the Scarecrow! However, there was nothing the girls could do but open their science books and follow their teacher's lesson.

For the rest of the morning, Alex tried to get Mr. Carpenter's attention. She wanted to ask him about the Scarecrow part. But her teacher seemed unusually busy and did not have time to speak to her.

"He never even came outside for recess!" Alex exclaimed to her friends at lunch. "It's like he doesn't want to see me or talk to me."

"And why should he?" said a nasty-sounding voice.

Alex gasped. She had not even noticed that Tyler was sitting at the end of the table.

"Mr. Carpenter just doesn't want to have to tell you that I got the part!" said Tyler.

"How do you know that, Tyler Forbes?" Janie cried, jumping up in anger.

"He doesn't know that," Julie said loudly. "He's just being a creep!"

"Oh, yeah?" Tyler shot back at Julie.

"Yeah!"

Alex, recovering from her shock, tried to pull Janie back down to her seat. "It's okay, Janie," she told her friend.

"But he said—" Janie pointed at Tyler.

"It's not worth fighting about." Alex tried to calm her friends. "We'll just get in trouble."

Indeed, one of the teachers on duty walked over to their table. "Is there something wrong, girls?"

"Oh, no," Alex replied and smiled sweetly.

"No, nothing wrong at all," Julie echoed.

Janie did not say anything. She blushed and looked down at the table.

The teacher nodded and moved away.

No one spoke further at the table. Alex was glad. She did not want Janie and Julie to get into a fight with Tyler. But what about Tyler? What if he was right? What if he did get the Scarecrow part?

At the next recess Mr. Carpenter asked Alex and Tyler to stay inside while the rest of the children went outside.

"We still do not know who will be the Scarecrow," the teacher told them. "We cannot choose between the two of you."

"You mean we're tied for the part?" Alex cried.

"That's exactly what I mean," Mr. Carpenter replied. He was perched on top of a desk with his long legs folded under him. "Mrs. Parrott and I are hoping that one of you will help us out," Mr. Carpenter went on. "We need someone to be the Master of Ceremonies and introduce the show to the audience. Of course, there wouldn't be as many speaking parts as the Scarecrow, but the Master of Ceremonies is an important position. Would one of you give up the Scarecrow part and be the Master of Ceremonies instead?"

Alex was too shocked to answer her teacher. What did he say? Give up the Scarecrow part?

Tyler looked down at his desk and scowled.

"Well, I thought I'd try," Mr. Carpenter sighed.

Alex stumbled outside for recess. Her thoughts jumped in confusion. Should she be the Master of Ceremonies? Should she let Tyler be the Scarecrow? But she had practiced so hard for the tryouts, and besides, Tyler was an absolute jerk—and who wanted to be nice to a jerk?

Alex's friends agreed. "Are you crazy, Alex?" Janie hollered when she heard the news. "Give Tyler the part? NEVER!"

Janie and Julie tried to convince Alex that holding out for the Scarecrow part was the right thing to do. But when Alex got home from school that afternoon, she asked her mother what she thought about it.

"Well, that's a tough one, Alex," Mother said. "I'm not sure what you should do."

"What do you mean?" Alex cried. "You don't think I should give Tyler the part, do you?"

"I think," Mother said slowly, "that the important question to ask is what does God want you to do?"

"I know," Alex admitted, "but what if He wants me to give up the Scarecrow part?"

"Then you should give it up," Mother said simply.

"But I want to be the Scarecrow really bad," Alex wailed.

"I know, honey," Mother put her arms around Alex, "but when God wants you to give up something, it usually means that He has something better in mind for you.''

"Something better?'' Alex frowned. "What could be better than being the Scarecrow in *The Wizard of Oz*?''

Mother laughed. "I understand how you feel, Alex. But just for a moment, think about Tyler and the other children at school. What would they think if you cheerfully gave Tyler the part with no complaints and no regrets?''

"They'd think I was crazy!'' Alex crossed her arms over her chest and frowned at her mother.

"Well, they might,'' Mother smiled. "Most people would not expect someone to give up a part out of the goodness of their heart.''

"Right,'' Alex agreed.

"But don't you see?'' Mother said excitedly. "That's being God's salt! That's flavoring the world! The world doesn't expect such a sacrifice. The world expects people to grab whatever they can for themselves. But that's not God's way. He wants His children to give to other people and to be kind to them. That's what makes us different. That's what makes us salt."

"Brussels sprouts!" Alex exclaimed, "I guess I never thought about it in that way. It almost makes me want to give up the part."

"Almost?" Mother questioned.

"Yeah, almost," Alex replied. "I mean, I don't know if I can give up the Scarecrow part. It's really special to me."

"I know, Alex," Mother said as she gave her a hug, "but there is something that could help you to do it. It is to remember another sacrifice when someone else gave up something special for you and for me."

"You mean when Jesus gave up His life for us, right?" Alex asked.

"Right," Mother replied.

By late evening, Alex was tired of worrying about the scarecrow part. She decided to go to bed and forget about it. Curling up beside her dog, T-Bone, Alex tried to relax. She was almost asleep when a sudden scratching noise made her sit upright in bed.

"What was that?" Alex asked the dog. T-Bone had raised his head and was staring at Alex. "Did you hear it too, T-Bone?" Alex whispered.

T-Bone continued to stare at Alex for a moment. Then he groaned and let his head fall back onto the bed.

"T-Bone!" Alex exclaimed. "Wake up! What if there's a burglar in here?"

The dog slowly opened one eye and then closed it again.

"Oh, well." Alex snuggled back under the

covers. "If you're not worried, then neither am I. It must have been my imagination." She yawned and settled her head on the pillow.

No sooner had Alex closed her eyes than SCRATCH! SCRATCH! S-C-R-A-P-E! went the noise again. It sounded as if it were coming from inside her closet.

"AHHHHH!" Alex cried and dove under the covers.

T-Bone was wide awake now. "WOOF! WOOF! WOOF! WOOF!" he barked and leaped from the bed. His fur bristled along his back. T-Bone growled ferociously as he made an attack on the closet door.

Alex shivered and shook under the covers of her bed. She didn't know what to do. She didn't want to come out from under the covers, yet she didn't want to stay in the bedroom. Finally, she made a dash for the door, her feet barely touching the floor.

"MOM! DAD!" Alex hollered from the top of the stairs. "HELP! THERE'S SOMETHING HORRIBLE UP HERE!"

CHAPTER 5

Tatters and Shreds

No sooner had Alex hollered downstairs than her father bounded around the stairway's curve and up to the top. Mother was right behind him.

"What's the matter?" they cried in alarm.

"There's something spooky in my closet!" Alex cried.

"Oh, give me a break!" said Barbara, coming out of her bedroom. "How can anyone study around here?"

Alex gave her sister the most horrid frown she could make. It was just like Miss Mushy to think only about herself when Alex's life could be in danger.

"There is something in my closet," Alex insisted. "It made a terrible scratching noise."

"Ooooooh!" Barbara cried. "I'll bet it's long, bloody fingernails!"

Rudy, who had come out of his bedroom to see what was going on, giggled at Barbara's words.

Alex stomped her foot and pointed toward her bedroom. "Go look and see. T-Bone heard it, too."

Father entered Alex's room. T-Bone still stood in front of the closet door, growling. Father moved up beside the dog.

"Do you think you ought to open the closet door?" Mother asked nervously.

"I'm going to listen at the door first," Father replied. He told the dog to be quiet and put his ear up against the closet door. "I do hear something scratching in there!" Father exclaimed after a minute.

"I told you!" Alex said triumphantly.

"Oh, dear," cried Mother.

"Does it sound like fingernails?" asked Barbara.

Father and Mother frowned at Barbara.

"Just kidding," she apologized.

Father listened at the door again. "It sounds like it could be a small animal."

"Oh, no." Mother said. "Do you think it could be a mouse?"

Just then, Alex noticed Rudy was nowhere in sight. That was strange. Rudy never missed out on any excitement. Where was he? Surely he hadn't gone back to bed.

"I'm going to open the closet door," Father announced.

"Be careful!" Mother called to him.

"One, two, three!" Father shouted. He flung open the closet door and jumped backwards.

Out in the hallway, Mother, Barbara, and Alex also jumped backwards. They got ready to run at a moment's notice.

However, nothing happened. Nothing ran out of the closet. Nothing could be seen inside the closet. The scratching noise had stopped.

"That's funny." Father scratched his head.

"It's not funny at all," Alex frowned. "It's spooky having something invisible scratching around in your closet."

"Now, Alex, don't worry. We'll find out what it was." Mother put her arm around Alex's shoulders.

"Hmmpf!" snorted Father as he peered into Alex's closet. "Something could live in this closet for weeks and you'd never find it."

"Well," Mother sighed, "let's start pulling things out."

"I wonder what's going to jump out at us," said Barbara. She pulled a cowboy boot, a dirty sneaker, an old tennis racket, and a shoe box filled with rocks out of Alex's closet. "Why do you have a box of rocks in your closet?" Barbara asked.

"It's my rock collection," Alex replied in a huff.

"And what's all this?" Father exclaimed, dragging out three more boxes.

"That's my shell collection, my bottle cap collection, and my eraser collection," Alex answered.

"Is there anything that you're not collecting?" Father asked.

"No," grinned Alex.

"How about turtles?" Barbara asked, yanking a particularly large box out of the closet.

"Turtles?" Alex frowned.

"Don't tell me," her sister snickered, "that you forgot about your turtle collection?"

Alex stared at her sister. What was Miss Mushy talking about? She walked over and stared into the big box. She blinked in surprise at seeing a rather large box turtle sitting in the center of the box. Around it lay tufts of grass. A partly spilled bowl of water sat in one corner.

"Brussels sprouts!" Alex exclaimed. "Where'd that turtle come from?"

"Just what every closet needs," commented Father.

"I guess now we know what made the scratching noises," said Mother.

"And it *was* fingernails," Barbara laughed, "or rather toenails. Turtle toenails!"

"But I didn't put it in my closet," Alex told them. She stared closer at the turtle. "Hey! That's Clementine!"

"Clementine?" her father exclaimed. "Are you sure?"

"Sure, I'm sure," Alex answered excitedly. "See that sort of triangle on her back?" She pointed to a set of lines on the turtle's shell. "And she should have a black dot on her belly." Alex flipped the turtle over on her back. "See, there's the dot! What did I tell you?"

"But if this is Clementine," Mother said slowly, "then it is Jason's turtle."

"And," Father picked up Mother's thought, "who else would put Jason's turtle in Alex's closet but . . . ?"

"RUDY!" they all shouted at once.

Alex beat everybody to Rudy's bedroom. "All right, Goblin," she hollered, flipping on the light switch. "What's the big idea putting Clementine in my closet?"

Rudy sat up in bed and blinked at her. "Huh?" He rubbed his eyes.

"It's no good pretending to be asleep, Goblin," Alex told him. "Why did you put Clementine in my closet?"

"Uh, well, I, uh," Rudy stammered. Both his parents and Barbara had joined Alex in his room.

"Answer the question, Rudy," said Father.

"I didn't mean for her to scratch and make noise and wake Alex up," Rudy tried to apologize.

"That's not a good answer to the question, Rudy," said Mother as she tapped her foot.

Rudy gulped. "Oh, well, I guess I put Clementine in Alex's closet to make Jason mad."

"And was it a right thing or a wrong thing to do?" Father asked Rudy.

"A wrong thing," Rudy admitted and hung his head.

"I think Rudy and I need to be alone for a while," Father told the rest of the family.

Mother nodded and guided Alex and Barbara out of Rudy's room.

As Mother pulled the door closed, Alex suddenly felt sorry for her brother. It was such an awful feeling to be in really big trouble. She knew she always felt like a bad person—not like her real self at all. And she wanted to hurry up and get the punishment over with so she could be forgiven and get back to being herself again.

"Brussels sprouts, that's funny!" Alex exclaimed out loud.

"What's funny?" Mother and Barbara both turned to look at her.

"Well, I just thought of something." Alex tried to explain what she was thinking. "Punishment can be kind of a good thing because after it's over, you feel okay again."

Mother smiled. "That's right," she agreed. "Punishment somehow releases us from the guilt we feel when we do something wrong. I guess it makes us feel as if we have paid for the wrong thing we have done."

Alex thought that the next week at school was the worst one in her life. Part of the time, she felt as if she should let Tyler be the Scarecrow, and the rest of the time she wanted to hold on to the part. Alex hated not being able to make the decision. She felt as if she were sinking in deep water, with two inner tubes on either side of her, and she didn't know which one to grab.

It was Wednesday morning and Alex was very upset. Mr. Carpenter had just told her that she and Tyler had to perform their scarecrow acts for him and Mrs. Parrott one more time. The teachers would then choose between them.

"It's just not fair," Alex complained to Janie at recess. "I don't have my costume here, and we have to do it today."

"That doesn't matter, Alex," Janie tried to comfort her friend. "Tyler doesn't have his costume, either."

"Oh, yes, he does," Alex sighed gloomily.

"He's had his costume here ever since the tryouts. He keeps it in his desk. I've seen him pull it out a few times."

"Really?" Janie exclaimed. "Are you sure?"

"Of course, I'm sure," Alex scowled. "His costume looks so good that Mrs. Parrott will pick him just because of it."

At lunchtime, Alex sat with Julie at their usual table in the lunchroom. Janie had not yet appeared.

"Where is Janie?" Alex asked Julie.

"I don't know," Julie replied.

"Well, she better get here pretty quick," Alex muttered, "because I want to know if she thinks I oughta do the flip."

"I think you ought to do the flip," said Julie. "Oh! Here comes Janie."

Janie hurried across the room to their table. Alex thought she looked worried or upset about something. "Where have you been?" Alex asked Janie.

"I had something I had to do," Janie replied, sounding quite a bit like Alex's mother.

Alex frowned but did not question Janie further. She was too worried about the flip at the end of her scarecrow act.

"Oh, yes, I think you should do the flip," Janie agreed with Julie. "And," Janie added, "don't worry about a thing. I'm positive you will get the part now."

Alex was about to ask her friend what made her so sure, but the bell rang, ending lunch period. Alex walked to the gymnasium where Mrs. Parrott and Mr. Carpenter were waiting for her and Tyler.

"Tyler isn't here yet, Alex, so why don't you go first," Mrs. Parrott suggested and pointed Alex to the stage.

Alex had barely started with a series of three somersaults when a sudden scream ripped through the gymnasium. Mrs. Parrott stopped the music and Alex fell flat in the middle of a roll.

Tyler rushed through the door and into the gym, waving his arms and yelling like a crazy person. He pointed at Alex. "See what she did to my costume? It's ruined!" he cried.

Alex and the teachers stared at Tyler in disbelief. His costume was shredded. It looked as if someone had whacked giant holes all over it. Even the hat—the beautiful, black, floppy hat—had been mutilated. It lay in tatters around Tyler's head.

It took Alex several seconds to realize that Tyler thought she had been the one to ruin his costume. "I didn't do it!" Alex called from the stage to Tyler. How could Tyler think that she would do such a thing?

"Oh, yes, you did!" Tyler hollered and would have rushed onto the stage if Mr. Carpenter had not grabbed him from behind.

"I think we need to take a walk to cool down," Mr. Carpenter said to Mrs. Parrott. "Would you please take Alex down to Mrs. Larson's office? Tyler and I will meet you there in a few minutes."

"Why are we going to Mrs. Larson's office?" Alex questioned her teacher.

Mr. Carpenter looked at her sternly. "I think we should discuss this matter in the principal's office."

"But I didn't do anything," Alex insisted.

"We will talk about it in Mrs. Larson's office," Mr. Carpenter repeated. He turned and led Tyler out of the room.

Mrs. Parrott did not say a word to Alex as they walked together to the principal's office.

"They think I did it," Alex exclaimed to herself. "Mr. Carpenter and Mrs. Parrott think that I cut holes in Tyler Forbes's scarecrow costume!"

CHAPTER 6

A Promise and a Sacrifice

"But I didn't do it!" Alex insisted. "I did not cut holes in Tyler's costume."

Alex was seated in Mrs. Larson's office with Mr. Carpenter, Mrs. Parrott, and Tyler.

"Alex, I really do want to believe you," Mrs. Larson replied. "But who else would have a reason to cut the holes in Tyler's costume?"

"I don't know," replied Alex, "but it wasn't me!" Suddenly, she put her hand over her mouth. "Uh oh," she gasped. Alex had just thought of someone else who had a reason to cut holes in Tyler's costume. Someone who wanted her best friend to get the Scarecrow part. Someone who had been missing at lunch for just enough time to do the job. Janie!

"Is something wrong, Alex?" Mrs. Larson asked.

Alex couldn't answer for a moment. Her face felt hot and her heart beat rapidly. Had Janie done such a thing? She couldn't tell Mrs. Larson that it had been her best friend, could she?

"Alex, are you all right?" There was concern in Mrs. Larson's voice.

Alex blinked and nodded. "I think I know who did it, but I can't tell you," she said in a small voice.

Everyone stared at Alex in surprise. Finally, Mr. Carpenter stood up. "I think I know who it is," he said and hurried out of the room.

It was not long before Mr. Carpenter returned and behind him, her face streaked with tears, walked Janie. "Janie has confessed to the crime," Mr. Carpenter told Mrs. Larson. "I thought you would want to talk to her."

"Yes, thank you," Mrs. Larson replied. "Alex, I am sorry that you were wrongly accused. You and Tyler may return to your classroom with Mr. Carpenter."

On the way back to their room, Alex said to Mr. Carpenter, "I just can't believe that Janie did that. That's not like Janie at all!"

"Janie wanted you to be the Scarecrow so badly that she did something terribly wrong to help you get it," Mr. Carpenter explained.

"Brussels sprouts," Alex frowned. "Janie ought to know that it doesn't work that way."

Mr. Carpenter looked puzzled. "What doesn't work what way?" he asked.

"Well, you can't do something bad and then expect something good to come out of it," Alex tried to explain. "It never works. Somehow, the bad always spoils the good."

Mr. Carpenter nodded in agreement. "Very well said."

Alex did not see Janie for the rest of the afternoon. She had to walk home alone with Rudy. She did not pay much attention to Rudy's chatter. She was too busy thinking about Janie and Tyler and the Scarecrow part.

"Alex!" Rudy suddenly shouted. "You're not even listening!"

"Huh?" Alex stared blankly at Rudy. "Sorry, what did you say?"

"I said," Rudy raised his voice, "that I bet creepy old Jason wishes he had somebody to walk with!"

"Creepy old Jason?" Alex repeated.

"Yeah." Rudy smirked and jerked his thumb over his shoulder.

Alex turned around and looked. Jason walked several yards behind them. He was all alone. Alex sighed. She wondered what she should say to her little brother.

"Goblin," Alex finally spoke, "you know how Jesus died for us on the cross?"

"Yeah?" Rudy looked surprised.

"Well, that was called a sacrifice." Alex chose her words carefully. "And I am going to make a sacrifice, too."

Rudy stopped dead in his tracks. "Do you mean you are going to get crucified, too?" he hollered.

"No, Goblin!" Alex cried and turned red. She looked around to make sure no one was listening.

"I'm going to make a different kind of sacrifice," Alex explained. "At least it will be a smaller one."

"What are you going to do?" Rudy asked.

"I'm going to give the Scarecrow part to Tyler," Alex said in a determined manner. As a matter of fact, it had not been until that moment that she had finally decided to do so.

"Really?" Rudy was surprised.

"Yes," Alex said firmly. "The whole thing has caused too much trouble." She told Rudy how Janie had cut holes in Tyler's costume and how Janie was now in big trouble.

"Poor Janie!" Rudy cried.

"And poor Tyler," Alex reminded him.

"Yeah, I guess I should feel sorry for Tyler even though he is a creep," said Rudy.

Alex eyed her younger brother. "So far on our walk home, you have called two people 'creeps' and one of them is your best friend."

"He is not!" Rudy shouted.

"He is too," Alex insisted. "And if you don't watch out, you might lose him as a friend forever."

Rudy stomped his way down the sidewalk. He was silent for so long that Alex began to think she had said something wrong.

"I guess I *am* getting tired of being mad at Jason," Rudy finally said. "When you're mad at your best friend, it sorta seems like you're mad at the whole world!"

"I know," Alex agreed.

"But I don't know what to do," Rudy moaned. "Jason's really mad at me . . . especially since I stole his turtle."

"You took Clementine back to Jason, didn't you?" Alex asked.

"Yeah, and Dad made me apologize," Rudy frowned. "You should have seen Jason's face. Boy, was he mad!"

"Well, he's had a few days to cool down," Alex pointed out.

Rudy shrugged.

"I thought maybe we could make a deal," Alex suggested.

Rudy looked interested. "What kind of a deal?"

"I'll promise to let Tyler have the Scarecrow

part if you will promise to make up with Jason.''

"Whew! I don't know!" Rudy shook his head.

"I'm not saying it will be easy, Goblin," Alex told him. "But those are both things that we need to do."

"Yeah." Rudy continued to shake his head. "I guess you're right."

"Deal?" Alex stuck out her hand.

"Deal!" Rudy grabbed her hand and shook it.

The next day, Alex did not waste any time. As soon as she got to school, she told Mr. Carpenter that he could give Tyler the Scarecrow part.

"Are you sure, Alex?" Mr. Carpenter asked.

"Yes," replied Alex. "There's been too much trouble over that part, and besides, I think that's what God wants me to do."

Mr. Carpenter raised his eyebrows. "Okay, I can't argue with that."

The news spread quickly. Alex's friends were disappointed, but also relieved. At least now the fighting with Tyler would be over.

Alex expected Tyler to thank her for giving up the part. But he did not. In fact, Tyler did not even look happy about Alex's decision.

"What's wrong with Tyler?" Julie asked Alex at lunchtime. "You'd think he would be glad to get the Scarecrow part."

"Yeah, but instead, he looks miserable," Janie added.

Alex shrugged. "Maybe Tyler found out that when you are mean to others, you really end up hurting yourself."

"Hmmpf!" replied Janie. "I guess I found that out yesterday."

The other girls laughed. Poor Janie! She was grounded for a whole month for cutting holes in Tyler's costume.

As soon as Alex got home from school that afternoon, she told her mother about giving the Scarecrow part to Tyler.

"Oh, Alex!" Mother cried. "That must have been so hard. I am very proud of you."

"It wasn't so bad," Alex replied. "The hard part was deciding to do it. I can't explain it, but I know I did the right thing."

"I think you did, too," Mother agreed. "Now what are you going to do in the musical?"

"I'm going to be the Master of Ceremonies," Alex said. "Mr. Carpenter said it was sort of like being the ringmaster at a circus. I get to introduce the show and say something after each act."

"Well, that sounds like an exciting part," Mother said encouragingly. "Maybe you will have more fun being the Master of Ceremonies than being the Scarecrow."

"Maybe," Alex sighed, "but I don't have as many speaking parts as the Scarecrow."

"Why don't you fix that?" said a voice behind Alex. She whirled around. Barbara stood there.

"What do you mean fix it?" Alex asked her sister.

"Fix it so that you have more speaking parts," said Barbara.

Alex and Mother stared at Barbara in surprise. "How?" they asked together.

Barbara shrugged. "Why not do a commercial or two?"

"A commercial or two?"

"Sure, you could make up a couple of commercials and do them at different times in your musical," Barbara explained.

"Brussels sprouts!" Alex cried. "That's a great idea!"

"If you want, I could help you figure them out," her sister offered.

"You would?" Alex jumped up and down in excitement.

Alex and Barbara spent the rest of the afternoon working on commercials. When Mother called them to dinner, the two sisters laughed and giggled their way down the stairs.

"What's so funny?" Father asked as they sat down at the dinner table.

"The commercial we made up is so funny!" Alex told her father. She then told him how she had given up the Scarecrow part and how she was going to be the Master of Ceremonies in the *Wizard of Oz*.

"Uh-huh." Father rubbed his chin. "Now wait, don't tell me . . . you are making a pizza commercial."

Alex laughed and shook her head.

"Ice-cream commercial?" Father tried again.

"No, Dad," Alex replied. "We are making up commercials about Kingswood School. The one we're writing now is about the food in the cafeteria." Alex laughed. "Boy, is it funny!"

"Alex?" Rudy leaned across the table and tapped her arm.

"What, Goblin?" Alex replied.

"Did you really give up the Scarecrow part today?"

"Yes, I did," answered Alex.

"Then there's something I have to do right now!" Rudy announced. "Please excuse me," he said, and before anyone could say a word, he dashed from the table and out the front door.

"Where's he going?" Father exclaimed.

Alex shrugged. "I guess he's going to Jason's."

"Jason's!" Father, Mother, and Barbara shouted together.

"Yeah, well, Rudy and I kind of made a deal," Alex explained. "You see, I promised to give up the Scarecrow part and he promised to make up with Jason. So, I'm sure he is going over to Jason's right now to apologize to him."

"This I have to see," said Father. He hurried to the front window. The others joined him.

They watched as Rudy walked through the yard and over to Jason's house. They saw Jason's mother open the door. Then, Rudy disappeared through the door and into the house.

"Brussels sprouts!" Alex shouted. "I wonder what's happening in there!"

"I'm sure Rudy is talking to Jason right now," said Mother. "They will be the best of friends before you know it."

"Yeah, unless Jason whacked Rudy before he could speak and Rudy got mad and whacked Jason back. They could be clobbering each other right now," Barbara pointed out.

"Oh, dear," Mother sighed.

Father laughed. "Well, whichever way it goes, I am sure we'll hear about it. Come on, let's go back to the dinner table. I'm starving!"

CHAPTER 7

T-Bone's Crash

When Alex asked Mrs. Parrott about having commercials in the musical, the music teacher thought that it was a wonderful idea.

"To tell you the truth, Alex," she whispered, "I am so grateful to you for giving the part to Tyler and keeping peace in the fourth grade, that I would probably let you do just about anything!"

"You mean it's okay to have my dog in one of the commercials?" Alex asked excitedly.

"As long as he behaves himself," Mrs. Parrott replied.

"Oh, he will!" promised Alex. That afternoon, she skipped home to tell Barbara the good news.

"Radical!" Barbara shouted when she heard it. "We better get to work on the float."

All week, the sisters labored at making a real parade float to sit on top of Alex's red wagon.

"What are you doing?" Rudy asked the girls on Saturday afternoon. They were sitting on the floor of the garage busily cutting purple circles out of contruction paper. Already-cut circles littered the floor of the garage.

"We're cutting out grapes, Goblin," Alex replied.

"You call those grapes?" Rudy scoffed.

"Yeah, why don't you help us?" Barbara suggested.

"No way!" Rudy replied. "Jason and I are going to practice baseball. Right, Jason?"

"Right!" Jason agreed. "Besides, those don't look like grapes to me. They look more like plums!"

The two boys giggled and ran off.

Barbara sighed, "I'm not sure if I'm glad they are friends again."

"Yeah, you kind of forget how smart-alecky they can be when they get together," agreed

Alex. "But you know, Jason's right. These don't look a whole lot like grapes."

"Oh, just wait until we paste the green stems on them," replied Barbara. "Then they'll look like grapes."

"We better decide how we are are going to attach the grapes to the wagon," Alex said. "I think we should make a kind of mountain in the back of the wagon and then cover it up with the grapes."

"Good idea," Barbara agreed. She pointed to a wheelbarrow full of dirt that Father was saving for a flower bed. "How about using dirt to make the mountain?"

"Super! I'll go ask Dad if we can use some of his dirt." Alex raced out to the end of the driveway where Father was busily painting some lawn furniture.

In a few moments, Alex reported to her sister. "He says we can use the dirt."

"Great!" Barbara stood up. "I'm tired of cutting out grapes. Let's load the dirt into the wagon. At least that will be something different to do."

It took several shovelfuls to fill the bed of the wagon. They piled the dirt as high as they could into a pyramid shape.

"I don't think we can put in anymore," Barbara decided.

"Hey, this is pretty heavy!" Alex exclaimed as she yanked on the wagon's handle. "I hope T-Bone can pull it."

"Maybe we should hook T-Bone up to it and see if he can pull it," said Barbara.

"Good idea!" Alex cried. "I'll go get him."

Returning with the big dog, Alex began to tie an end of his leash to the wagon handle. "No, no, no," Barbara waved her arms. "T-Bone needs a harness of some kind. You know, like they put on horses when they pull a stagecoach or something."

"Brussels sprouts, where can we get a harness?" Alex asked.

"I think we can make one out of his leash," Barbara said. She carefully wound T-Bone's leash around his chest and behind his front legs. She then fastened the "harness" to the wagon with rope.

"There!" she said proudly.

"Brussels sprouts!" Alex was impressed. "T-Bone, you look like a mule ready to pull a load of gold from the mine."

T-Bone was not at all pleased with his harness. He tried to bite through its straps.

"T-Bone, cut it out!" Alex cried. "You are going to be a star in one of my commercials. Now come on. We have to practice!"

Alex tried to get the big dog to move forward. "Here, T-Bone, come on, boy, let's go!" She whistled, clapped her hands, and pulled on the harness. Nothing worked. T-Bone would not move.

"Oh, T-Bone, it can't be that heavy!" Alex said to the dog. T-Bone gazed mournfully back at the wagon load.

"Maybe if I pushed the wagon from behind, he would get the idea," Barbara suggested.

"Okay," Alex agreed. Barbara gingerly pushed the wagon into the backside of T-Bone. The big dog took a step forward. Barbara pushed again. The dog took two steps forward.

"It's working," Alex called over her

shoulder. "Come on, T-Bone, keep going! Let's go, T-Bone!"

Alex and the dog and the wagon proceeded slowly out of the garage and down the driveway. Alex waved to her father who looked up from his painting job. Father laughed and waved his paint brush at her.

The wagon picked up speed as it rolled down the driveway's slope. T-Bone trotted beside Alex.

Suddenly, a squirrel popped out of nowhere and ran across the driveway right under T-Bone's nose!

"Oh, no!" Alex yelled. She knew that T-Bone considered it his job to keep all squirrels up in trees where they belonged. Any squirrel that dared to touch ground while T-Bone was around would be chased right back up its tree.

Just as Alex feared, T-Bone leaped for the squirrel that dashed across the driveway. The leash jerked out of Alex's hands. T-Bone chased after the squirrel, bouncing the wagon along behind him.

Alex could see the panic spread over her father's face as the squirrel, T-Bone, and the wagon full of dirt rushed toward him and his freshly painted lawn furniture.

On reaching Father, the squirrel made a giant lunge and flew over two lawn chairs. But it landed hard on a table, leaving its tracks all across the wet paint.

T-Bone slid sideways into Father, knocking both of them to the ground. WHAM! BANG! KLUNK! The wagon crashed into the furniture and tipped over, throwing dirt all over the furniture.

Alex stood as if cemented to the center of the driveway. Her mouth hung open but she couldn't say a word. Barbara stood a little to one side. Her hands covered her face.

"ALEXANDRIA BRACKENBURY!" Father roared. "COME AND GET THIS DOG OFF OF ME!"

Alex raced to the end of the driveway. "T-BONE! T-BONE!" she cried and threw her arms around the big dog's neck. "Are you hurt?"

"T-Bone?" her father exclaimed. "I would think you might be a little more concerned about your father!"

"Oh, sorry, Dad," Alex mumbled. She helped her father and T-Bone stand up. They both seemed to be all right.

"I guess we caused sort of a mess," said Barbara as she came up behind Father and Alex.

"That's the understatement of the year," replied Father. He stared at the furniture on the driveway. Instead of white, one chair was now completely black with dirt. The rest of the furniture was polka-dotted with clumps of dirt.

"Well, I guess you girls know what you'll be doing this afternoon," Father stated.

"What?" Alex asked in a small voice.

"Hold out your hand," Father directed. He slapped a paint brush into Alex's outstretched hand.

"Oh," Alex sighed and rolled her eyes at Barbara.

"Wash the dirt off the furniture before you paint it," Father told them. He reached down to pat T-Bone's head. "Come on, boy. You and I are going to watch the ball game." Father waved to Alex and Barbara as he and T-Bone disappeared inside the house.

"If I hear 'Over the Rainbow' one more time today," Alex told Janie, "I think I will scream!"

Members of Alex's class were rehearsing in the gymnasium. The girl who was playing Dorothy had just sung "Over the Rainbow" several times in a row.

Alex and Janie were at the back of the stage putting the finishing touches on the background scenery. Alex was filling in the jagged outlines of bricks with bright yellow paint.

"The yellow brick road is all finished," she hollered to Mr. Carpenter.

"Very good," her teacher replied. He walked across the stage to inspect the scenery.

Suddenly Mrs. Parrott called, "ALEX! We need you to rehearse your speaking parts."

"Brussels sprouts!" Alex exclaimed. She handed Mr. Carpenter her paint brush and ran to the front of the stage.

"Yuck!" Mr. Carpenter yelled. Yellow paint ran off the paint brush and into the palm of his hand.

"Alex," Mrs. Parrott directed from the front of the stage, "pretend that your audience is here and you are speaking to it."

Alex nodded and reached for the big microphone set up at the front of the stage. She gripped it excitedly. This was the first time that she got to say all of her lines, from start to finish. She was even going to run through her commercials for Mrs. Parrott. Of course, she couldn't do them quite properly without T-Bone or the wagon full of grapes.

"Ladies and gentlemen! Boys and girls! Welcome to this year's fourth grade musical production—*The Wizard of Oz*!" Alex called through the microphone in a voice that was loud and strong. She had memorized her speech well and felt confident. As Master of Ceremonies, she proudly wore an old derby hat that had been in the Brackenbury family for years.

Everyone in the gymnasium stopped to

listen. No one had heard the Master of Ceremonies speak before.

"Our cast of characters includes Margaret Terry as Dorothy," Alex announced. She paused and her classmates clapped and cheered for Margaret. "And Tyler Forbes as the Scarecrow," Alex went on. She waited for the children to clap for Tyler, but they did not do so. No one, not even Tyler's friends, cheered for him. As a matter of fact, Alex heard a few low boos and hisses.

Alex glanced at Tyler. He stared straight ahead and did not look at anyone. Mrs. Parrott caught Alex's eye and motioned for her to go on with her lines.

Alex opened her mouth to speak but, at that moment, a low rumble began from the back of the gym. It grew louder and louder. Looking around, Alex gasped. The giant board that she and Janie had painted just a few minutes before was falling! And it was falling right on top of Janie!

"JANIE!" Alex screamed, "GET OUTA THE WAY!"

CHAPTER 8

Locked in the Gym

Alex stared in fright as she watched the scenery fall closer and closer to Janie. Janie's face was terribly white. It looked as if she were too scared to move. Then, just in time, Mr. Carpenter grabbed Janie's arm and pulled her out of the way. WHAM! The board hit the floor face down.

"Whew!" Alex shuddered in relief.

"I hope the paint was dry," Mrs. Parrott remarked as she stared down at the back of the board. The front—the side on which the scenery was painted—lay flat against the floor.

"I know the paint was still wet," Janie answered gloomily. She held her wet paint brush up for Mrs. Parrott to see.

"Well, let's get it up off the floor and see

what damage has been done," Mr. Carpenter sighed as he grabbed a corner of the board.

"Oh, no," everyone groaned when they saw the scenery. Parts of it were badly smeared. The yellow brick road looked as if someone had flung gobs of paint at the bricks.

"And I was so careful to stay inside the lines," moaned Alex.

"I just don't know what we are going to do," worried Mrs. Parrott. "Tomorrow is dress rehearsal. We can't possibly paint another board of scenery tonight."

"My sister can," Alex volunteered.

"What?" Mrs. Parrott exclaimed. Everyone turned to stare at Alex.

"Well, she can," Alex insisted. "Barbara's really good at art. She's going to be an artist when she grows up."

Mrs. Parrott smiled. "But, Alex, would your sister want to paint an entire board of scenery tonight?"

"Oh, sure," Alex replied. "She likes to do anything that has art in it. We could come after school and do it."

"Really?" Mrs. Parrott began to look hopeful.

"It sounds like a good idea to me," said Mr. Carpenter. "Right after school, check to see if your sister will do it."

Alex and Janie rushed home from school that afternoon. They hurried so fast that Rudy and Jason could hardly keep up with them. All four of them burst into the Brackenbury home and huffed and puffed their way to the kitchen.

Alex breathed a sigh of relief to see Barbara sitting at the kitchen table. She had been afraid that her sister might have stopped at a friend's house on her way home from school. "Barbara!" Alex cried. "We need your help! We have an emergency!"

Barbara calmly continued to lick the icing out of the middle of the cookie she was eating. "What's the problem?" she mumbled. "Did your softball fall in the sewer again?"

"No," Alex sighed. "This is a real problem." She and Janie told Barbara about the board of scenery falling to the floor during rehearsal that afternoon.

"And I told Mrs. Parrott that you were a really good artist and that you could paint us another scenery board," Alex told her sister.

"Thanks a lot," Barbara mumbled through another cookie.

"And Mrs. Parrott and Mr. Carpenter said it would be really neat if you would do it," Alex added hopefully.

"Radical," Barbara replied and reached for a third cookie.

"But it has to be done right away—like today." Alex clenched her teeth in anxiety.

"Uh-huh," her sister mumbled.

"Well, will you do it?" Alex almost screamed in frustration.

Barbara shrugged and stood up. "It might be interesting," she said. "I'll go get my paints."

Alex waited until her sister left the kitchen, then collapsed in a kitchen chair. "Teenagers!" she exclaimed to Janie. "You sure have to do some fast talking to get them to do anything!"

Janie agreed with Alex, and then sighed. "I'd better go home. If I wasn't grounded, you know I'd help paint the scenery," she said.

It wasn't too long before Alex and Barbara hurried down the Juniper Street hill. Rudy and Jason trotted along beside them.

When they reached Kingswood Elementary, the children rushed through a back door that led into the gymnasium.

"We oughta go tell Mrs. Parrott that we're here," Alex suggested. "She's probably in the music room."

"Right," Barbara agreed, "but first, help me set up my paints so I can get started. It's going to take quite awhile to paint all of this," she said eyeing the scenery board.

Alex helped Barbara arrange her paints. Barbara began to sketch an outline of the yellow brick road onto the backside of the board as Alex watched. A sudden loud slam made both girls jump.

"Goblin! What are you doing?" Alex demanded.

"Closing the door so we have some privacy," Rudy answered in a grown-up way.

"Rudy, if you and Jason cannot behave yourselves in here, you will have to go home,"

said Barbara, annoyed. The loud slam had caused her to smear part of the drawing.

"Well, we can't go home anyway even if you told us to," Rudy informed his older sister.

"And why not?" Barbara frowned.

"Because the door won't open," Rudy answered triumphantly.

"Well, push on it," Barbara told him.

"I can't." Rudy shrugged his shoulders. "It's locked!"

"Locked!" Barbara repeated, and looked at Alex in alarm.

"It can't be locked, Goblin," Alex scoffed. "We just came in through that door." She jumped off the stage and ran over to the door.

"He's right," she called after testing the door. "It's locked! Now how did that happen?"

"When we came in through the door, it was standing open," Barbara pointed out. "The door shouldn't lock automatically when it's closed. But when the boys slammed it, it must have jammed."

"Way to go, Goblin!" Alex shouted at Rudy.

"How was I supposed to know it would do that?" Rudy whined.

"Try the other door." Barbara pointed in the opposite direction.

"Oh, yeah," Alex cried hopefully. She ran to the other side of the room.

"It's no use," she hollered, "this one won't open, either!"

"Oh, great!" exclaimed Barbara. "We are officially trapped in the gym!"

Alex could not help but grin. "I always

wondered what it would be like to be locked in somewhere. I wonder who will come and rescue us?"

"Maybe Superman," suggested Rudy.

"Oh, brother," Barbara sighed. "Of all people, why did I have to get stuck in the gym with you guys?"

"Just lucky, I guess," Rudy told her.

"Hmmmpf," Barbara sniffed. "Well, at least Mom knows where we are."

"Oh, good, I'm glad you told her," said Alex.

"Wait a minute," Barbara cried, "I thought you told her."

"No, I didn't tell her. I thought you did," Alex exclaimed in alarm.

"Wonderful!" Barbara threw her hands up in the air. "We're locked in the gym and nobody knows where we are!"

The others were silent. They stared at one another with wide-open eyes. Then, Alex began to giggle. One by one, the others joined her until they were all laughing hilariously, even Barbara.

"Whew," gasped Barbara after a few minutes. "I'm not sure why we are laughing but it made me feel a lot better."

"Yeah," Alex agreed. "Like Dad always says, 'If there's nothing else you can do, you might as well laugh.' "

"I guess he's right," said Barbara, "but there *is* something else we can do."

"What's that?" Alex asked.

"Let's paint the scenery before we are rescued by Superman." Barbara winked at Rudy.

Alex climbed back onto the stage to help Barbara. Rudy and Jason went off to a corner of the gym to play. Soon, the girls heard strange noises from the boys' corner.

"Eeeeeeerrrrrrrrrrreeeeeeerrrrr!"

"Goblin! What are you doing?" Alex called from the stage.

"We are the police and we're chasing bank robbers!" Jason shouted over Rudy's siren noise.

"Eeeeeeerrrrrrrrrrreeeeeeerrrrr! POW! POW! BLAM!"

"Brussels sprouts," Alex sighed. The girls shook their heads at the boys.

"All right! I got you covered! Come on out with your hands up!" Rudy suddenly cried.

Alex and Barbara began to giggle at Rudy, but they stopped at once when a strange voice shouted from the other side of the room. "Oh, no you don't! I got you covered! You kids come out of there right now!"

A man stood in the shadowy area by the door, his hands on his hips. It took a few minutes before she recognized Mr. Whitney, the custodian of Kingswood Elementary.

"Mr. Whitney!" Alex called. "Don't you remember me?"

"Eh?" the custodian stared at the stage.

"I'm the one who got the softball stuck up on the roof," Alex reminded him.

"By golly," Mr. Whitney snapped his fingers, "so it is you. But what are you doing here so late after school?"

Alex told Mr. Whitney about painting the scenery. She also told him how they had accidentally been trapped in the gym.

Mr. Whitney rubbed his chin. "But who was making those awful screeching noises over the intercom?" he asked.

"Awful screeching noises?" Alex repeated, puzzled.

"Yeah, you know, the 'POW POWS' and the 'Come out with your hands up!' " said Mr. Whitney.

The girls looked at Rudy and Jason and giggled. "Uh, we were just playing and making noises," Rudy stammered.

Mr. Whitney rubbed his chin again. He walked over to the corner where the boys had been playing. "Did you, by any chance, push this button up here?" He pointed to a square speaker mounted on the wall.

"Yes," Rudy admitted, "that was our police car radio."

"Well, when it's not being used as a police car radio, it's used as an intercom," Mr. Whitney told the boys. "Your screeches and 'POW POW's' echoed all over the school building. I'd say you 'bout scared Mrs. Larson to death!"

"Mrs. Larson?" the children exclaimed in alarm.

Mr. Whitney chuckled. "Don't worry," he said, "Mrs. Larson will understand. And don't be too angry with your little brother," he told Barbara and Alex. "If he hadn't made so much noise, you might have spent the night in the gym without anyone knowing it!"

Mr. Whitney used the intercom to tell Mrs. Larson what had happened. Alex breathed a sigh of relief to know that the principal was not angry as she ran to the school office to telephone her mother. Mother said she would call Jason's mother.

In about an hour, Mother came to see how they were getting along. A little while later, Father came to the gym. Soon after that, the board was finished and the paints and brushes cleaned and put away.

Alex breathed a happy sigh as she climbed into the family station wagon and sat next to Barbara in the backseat. Her sister had done a great job on the scenery. It looked even better than before!

Alex wished she could tell Barbara just how thankful she was for all of her hard work on the scenery, but that would sound too stupid. "Thanks," was all Alex said, hoping that somehow her sister would know just how much she meant it.

"Sure, Short Stuff," Barbara replied and squeezed Alex's knee. It was the kind of squeeze that let Alex know that her sister understood.

CHAPTER 9

The Grape Mountain

"Bye, Mom," Alex called over her shoulder. "Don't forget to bring T-Bone to school this afternoon!"

"Okay, Alex," Mother called back. "Be careful with that wagon."

Today was dress rehearsal, and Alex and Janie had to pull the "mountain of grapes" float to school.

Barbara and Alex had worked hard on the grape mountain. They had decided not to use a dirt mountain, but had wrapped several layers of foam rubber into a cone shape. They then used glue and tape to attach the purple construction-paper circles to the cone. Green yarn draped around the grapes made perfect stems.

The grape mountain measured a little over four feet tall and, after being anchored to the bed of Alex's wagon, the entire float stood over six feet.

Starting off to school, Alex pulled the wagon over the crest of the Juniper Street hill. Almost immediately, she had to pull back on the handle of the wagon to keep it from shooting down the hill.

"Uh, Alex," said Janie as she ran alongside the wagon, "if this thing starts to fall, I don't think I can catch it!"

"Brussels sprouts, Janie!" Alex exclaimed, "Don't talk like that! It can't fall! You just can't let it fall!"

"Hey, Alex, this is neat!" Jason cried as he bounded over to them.

"It would be neater if T-Bone were pulling it," Rudy said, joining Jason on the sidewalk.

"Very funny, Goblin," Alex retorted. "You know T-Bone can't pull the grape mountain all the way to school. Mom's gonna bring him to school later so he can pull it at dress rehearsal."

"Hey, you guys!" Rudy called to a group of

neighborhood children walking behind them. "Look at my sister's grape mountain!"

"Oh, no," Alex moaned. "Don't touch it," she shouted as a sudden wave of children surrounded the mountain.

"What is it?" one boy asked, wrinkling his nose.

"It's a purple pyramid," grinned another.

"Naw, it's too lumpy to be a pyramid," argued a girl.

"It's supposed to be a mountain full of grapes," Alex tried to explain. "You know, like a float in a parade."

"A float!" They all laughed. "Did you use grape soda in your float?"

Alex sighed and continued to steer the wagon slowly and carefully down the hill.

"Look, Alex!" Janie called from the back of the wagon. "Look behind us!"

Alex turned her head. Rudy, Jason, and the other children were marching single file behind the grape mountain.

"You said it was like a float in a parade," Rudy called to Alex. "Here's the parade!"

Alex laughed. It was fun to be the head of a parade, especially when you were pulling the main attraction.

Other children joined the parade as it made its way down Juniper Street. "This is getting embarrassing," Janie called, as the line that marched behind Alex and the mountain stretched longer and longer.

They had reached the bottom of the hill and had turned right, going along another street that took them to the crosswalk in front of Kingswood Elementary School.

"Brussels sprouts!" Alex exclaimed as she saw that the parade now stretched for over two blocks. And still more children were coming. They marched behind the mountain pretending to play imaginary musical instruments or twirling imaginary batons. Rudy pranced up and down the parade line, blowing a pretend trombone.

When Alex reached the crosswalk, she tried not to look at the safety patrol. The older girl stared wide-eyed at the mountain and the parade behind it.

At that moment, the traffic light turned green. The safety patrol walked to the middle of the crosswalk and held out her flag. Alex, with Janie's help, rolled the grape mountain over the curb and into the street.

The line of children followed the mountain, dancing and playing their pretend band instruments. The cars that were waiting on both sides of the crosswalk honked merrily at the parade and their drivers cheered and waved to the children.

There was such a lot of noise and excitement

that Mrs. Larson and several teachers hurried outside the school building to see what was happening. Mr. Carpenter quickly joined the safety patrol in the middle of the street to make sure that all of the children in the parade crossed the street safely.

Alex pulled the mountain slowly up the school driveway and into the front door of the school. She grinned from ear to ear. Who would have thought that her grape mountain would cause such wonderful excitement? Janie walked behind Alex, her hands covering her embarrassed face.

The parade continued to follow Alex and the mountain until she parked the wagon in the music room. Then everyone scurried to their classrooms.

T-Bone performed well at dress rehearsal that afternoon. He pulled the grape mountain around the stage as a part of Alex's first commercial. Of course, Alex walked beside her dog to keep him in line.

A crowd of children surrounded T-Bone

after rehearsal. "He's a neat dog," somebody told Alex.

"Thanks," Alex replied proudly.

"Just think," said a boy, "if Alex had been the Scarecrow instead of the Master of Ceremonies, then we wouldn't have any neat commercials in our play."

"And we wouldn't have T-Bone in our play," shouted someone else.

Alex grinned with pleasure. She was glad to be the Master of Ceremonies. It was turning out to be more fun than the Scarecrow part.

Looking around, Alex was surprised to see Tyler watching her. He scowled and looked terribly unhappy. "I wonder what's wrong with him?" Alex asked herself.

When her mother came to pick Alex and T-Bone up after dress rehearsal, Alex said, "You know it's funny how things turn out sometimes."

"What do you mean?" Mother asked.

"Well, I'm really glad I'm not the Scarecrow, because I like being the Master of Ceremonies," Alex explained. "I have a lot of speaking parts and the commercials are fun to do. And today, the other kids said that they are glad that I am the Master of Ceremonies and not the Scarecrow.''

Mother nodded. ''It seems to have worked out pretty well.''

''Yes,'' Alex replied, ''it worked out good for me, but it doesn't seem to have worked out for Tyler.''

''Why not?'' Mother asked, surprised.

''All Tyler does is frown and look mad,'' Alex replied. ''I don't understand it. He got what he wanted. He got to be the Scarecrow.''

''That's true,'' Mother replied, ''but Tyler got what he wanted in the wrong way. No one can find real happiness if they hurt other people to get it.''

''Do you mean that it's more important how we get something than getting it?'' Alex asked her mother.

''Exactly.'' Mother smiled. ''Tyler didn't care one thing about you or your feelings. All he cared about was getting the Scarecrow part for himself.''

Alex nodded in agreement.

"But, even though you wanted to be the Scarecrow, you did the right thing by giving up the part to help out Tyler and your teachers," said Mother. "It's no wonder that you feel good and Tyler feels bad."

"Yeah," Alex agreed, "but I also gave up the Scarecrow part because that's what God wanted me to do."

"Yes," Mother added, "and that's the best reason of all. God knew you were strong enough to make that sacrifice. And making sacrifices for others is as close as we can come to being like Jesus."

"But it doesn't really seem like much of a sacrifice now," Alex said, "because I'm happy being the Master of Ceremonies."

Mother laughed. "God blesses us when we sacrifice something for Him. I think getting the Master of Ceremonies part was God's way of saying, 'Good job, Alex.' "

CHAPTER 10

A Double Blessing

The next morning, Alex leaped out of bed. This was it! This was the day of the musical!

Alex dressed so fast that she beat everyone down the stairs to the breakfast table. Everyone except Mother, of course.

"Well, I can tell that this is an unusual day," Mother chuckled when she saw Alex. On weekdays, Father was the first one to the breakfast table, followed by Rudy. Barbara and Alex tied for last place.

Alex ate her breakfast quickly and gathered her books together. "Don't forget to bring T-Bone and my costume to school," she reminded her mother.

Mother had made Alex a pair of black-and-white-striped pants to match a black-and-white-striped suit jacket. Alex planned to wear a bright red shirt under the jacket and gold suspenders. Father's old derby hat would top off her Master of Ceremonies outfit.

Just then the doorbell rang. Alex jerked open the door. "Janie! You're fifteen minutes early!" she cried.

"I know," Janie said breathlessly, "but I can't help it. I'm too excited!"

"Me, too." Alex grinned. She grabbed her backpack and she and Janie ran down the Juniper Street hill and all the way to school.

The morning dragged. Alex thought the clock would never make it to nine . . . ten . . . or eleven. Lunch came and went. So did the second recess. Finally, at two o-clock, Mr. Carpenter dismissed his class to go put on their costumes and set up the stage.

"Oh, Alex, I'm so nervous!" Janie exclaimed as she helped Alex pull her gold suspenders into place.

"Now, Janie, don't worry." Alex tried to calm her friend. "Just remember to come off stage after the Munchkins sing so that you will have time to put on your raisin costume before the first commercial."

"But why do I have to lead the raisin line?" Janie wailed. "Why do I have to be first?"

"Because you are the best," Alex reassured her. "You'll do great, Janie."

Alex had taped a special version of the song, "I Heard It Through the Grapevine" to use in the first commercial. She and Barbara had made up special words to the song.

"All you have to do is lead the line of raisins onto the stage in time to the music," Alex reminded Janie.

"I know, I know," Janie sighed.

"Then I'll lead T-Bone and the grape mountain out onto the stage," Alex added. "I just hope everything goes okay. I guess there aren't any squirrels in here for T-Bone to chase!"

When it was time to announce the beginning of the show, Mrs. Parrott signaled to Alex.

"Ladies and gentlemen! Boys and girls! Welcome to this year's musical production . . . *The Wizard of Oz!*"

Alex's voice rang out through the microphone. Out of the corner of her eye, she could see her father wink and her mother smile. Just knowing that they were there helped Alex to have confidence.

To Alex, the first part of the musical went fast. Dorothy did a fine job of singing "Over the Rainbow." Janie and the other Munchkins danced and sang. The tornado dropped Dorothy's house on the Wicked Witch of the East, and before Alex knew it, it was time for the first commercial.

Holding her breath, Alex pushed "play" on the tape recorder. Janie and the other raisins formed a line and danced out onto the front half of the stage.

"OoooohOOOOOOHwooooohWoooooH!
I heard it on the grapevine,
that Kingswood School is so fine!"

The raisin line weaved back and forth across the stage, moving their arms and legs to the beat of the music. The audience cheered and clapped their approval.

At the end of the second chorus, Alex and T-Bone appeared on the back half of the stage. T-Bone was "harnessed" to the grape mountain. He had a bright purple bow tied around his neck and another one around his tail. The audience laughed when they saw T-Bone.

Alex gently tugged on T-Bone's harness to move the dog forward, but the big Labrador would not budge.

"Come on, T-Bone," Alex whispered. She tugged again, this time a little harder. The dog still would not move. He looked at the audience and hid his head behind Alex's legs.

"T-Bone!" Alex whispered frantically. "Whoever heard of a dog having stage fright?"

A few low chuckles sounded from the audience. Alex did not know what to do. Then, suddenly, she heard her father whistle softly to T-Bone. It was the same whistle Father used every day to call the big dog to him.

T-Bone's head jerked around from behind Alex. He pricked up his ears and began to walk toward the audience.

Alex caught hold of T-Bone's harness and had no further trouble moving the dog and the grape mountain around on the stage behind the raisin line. The audience clapped loudly for Alex, T-Bone, and the raisins.

During the second half of the musical, Alex watched Tyler dance and sing in the cornfield. Although Tyler acted the part of the Scarecrow, Alex had the feeling that something was missing. There was something that wasn't quite right. It wasn't until the Scarecrow met the Tin Man and the Lion that Alex thought she knew what it was. The Scarecrow seemed sad. He didn't have the bouncy, carefree steps that he should have. There was no joy in his voice when he spoke or sang.

Alex was concentrating so much on Tyler that she almost missed the time for her second commercial. The stage was completely empty when Alex hurried to her spot in the center of it.

Clasping her hands behind her back, Alex began to recite the funny poem that Barbara had helped her to write:

"The Kingswood School Cafeteria"

If you would like a special treat,
Something yummy and good to eat,
Whether you want it sour or sweet,
Come to the Kingswood cafeteria.

The food they serve is not too old,
Grilled ham and cheese, stiff 'n' cold,
Brown apples, hot dogs green with mold,
Come to the Kingswood cafeteria.

Burnt fried chicken, soggy french fries,
Applesauce lumps and runny cream pies,
All so good, you won't believe your eyes,
Come to the Kingswood cafeteria.

The salads are dry, the hamburgers
    black,
They taste so good—just like a Big Mac,
Once you try it, you'll have to come
    back,
Back to the Kingswood cafeteria.

By the time Alex finished reciting her poem,
the gym was in an uproar. The audience

119

laughed so loud and so long that Alex was afraid they might never stop. She grinned at Barbara in the audience. Their poem was a great success.

All too soon for Alex, the last act of the musical ended. Everyone clapped and cheered for the actors and actresses as they came on stage for their final bows, but no one got more applause than Alex.

"Alex, I think your commercials were the biggest hit of the show!" Mrs. Parrott exclaimed.

"Good job, Alex!" Mr. Carpenter patted her on the shoulder.

The children climbed down from the stage to join their families. Everyone congratulated each other noisily. Parents formed little groups and talked and talked and talked. The children ran from one group to another or formed their own groups.

Father took charge of T-Bone. Alex could hear Father in the background, his big booming laugh filling the gym. He was telling a group of people the story of T-Bone and the squirrel and the lawn furniture.

"Uh, Alex," said a voice at her side.

Alex was surprised to see Tyler standing beside her.

"I, uh, well," Tyler stammered and looked down at his feet. Suddenly, he grabbed her hand and shook it. "You did a good job, Alex," he blurted and walked away quickly.

For a moment, Alex was too surprised to say anything. Then, she ran after him and called, "So did you, Tyler!" She saw him smile back at her.

"What did that dorky Tyler want?" Janie asked as she and Julie came up to Alex.

"He's not so bad," Alex smiled.

"Hmmmpf!" Janie snorted. "Did he ever thank you for letting him have the Scarecrow part?"

"Well," Alex said, slowly nodding her head, "I think he just did—in his own way."

Just then a soft wet nose snuggled Alex's hand. "T-Bone!" she cried, flinging her arms around her dog's neck. "You did just super on stage!"

"Well, I certainly wish I could get hugs like the dog gets," Father teased loudly.

"Oh, Dad," Alex sighed.

Her father chuckled. "I have something for you," he said and pulled an envelope out of his pocket. He handed it to Alex.

"What is it?" she asked, turning the envelope over and over in her hands.

"Why don't you open it and find out," Father suggested.

Alex tore open the envelope and pulled out five tickets. On each ticket was written the words, "Los Angeles."

All at once, Alex's face lit up. "Are these airplane tickets?" she cried.

"Yes," replied Father.

"To Los Angeles?" Alex cried again.

"Yes." Father smiled. "Because you did such a good job on your commercials, I thought that you might want to go and see how they make commercials in Hollywood." He paused for a moment. "I thought we might take the rest of the family along," he added with a wink.

"Can we go to Disneyland, too?"

"You bet!" answered Father.

"BRUSSELS SPROUTS!" Alex shouted and leaped into her father's arms. She hugged him tightly around the neck.

"So I finally do get a hug like T-Bone," Father joked.

"Aw, Dad," Alex laughed and laid her head on his shoulder. "I guess Mom was right," she mumbled into her father's ear.

"How was Mom right, Firecracker?" her father asked.

"Well, she said that if God wants you to give up something, then He usually has something better in mind for you. And He did. He had the Master of Ceremonies part in mind for me and that turned out to be better than the Scarecrow part."

"Uh-huh," Father agreed.

"Then Mom also said that God blesses us when we sacrifice something for Him. Well, I got a double blessing! I got to be the Master of Ceremonies and I also got tickets to go to California!"

Father laughed and squeezed Alex tighter. "God loves you, Firecracker," he said.

Amen.

SHOELACES AND BRUSSELS SPROUTS

One little lie, but BIG trouble!

When Alex lies to her mom about losing her shoelaces, it doesn't seem like a big deal. But how do you replace special baseball laces when you don't have any money and you're not allowed to go to the store alone? A big softball game is coming up, and Alex knows the coach won't let her pitch in shoes without laces—or in cowboy boots!

Every kid gets into the predicaments that Alex does—ones that start out small and mushroom. Readers will learn from Alex's mistakes and understand that they have the same sources of help that she turns to: A God who loves them and wants to help them, and parents who understand.

Other books in the Alex Series . . .

2 *French Fry Forgiveness*—Sometimes making friends is harder than making enemies.

3 *Hot Chocolate Friendship*—Is winning first place as important to Alex as being a friend?

4 *Peanut Butter and Jelly Secrets*—Obeying her parents (even in little things) beats the awful results of disobeying.

Available at your local Christian bookstore.

David C. Cook Publishing Co.
850 N. Grove Ave.
Elgin, IL 60120

CHERRY COLA CHAMPIONS

It's soccer season!

Alex can't imagine anyone not loving soccer until Lorraine joins her team. Lorraine can't run or kick. And no one wants to play with her.

How does that make Lorraine feel? Alex wonders. . . . But watch out when Alex decides to teach Lorraine soccer! Then maybe the kids will like Lorraine better. How can she lose with Alex as her coach?

Every kid gets into the predicaments that Alex does—ones that start out small and mushroom. Readers will learn from Alex's mistakes and understand that they have the same sources of help that she turns to: A God who loves them and parents who understand.

More books in the Alex series...

Mint Cookie Miracles (About Prayer)
Cherry Cola Champions
   (About Compassion)
The Salty Scarecrow Solution
   (About Unselfishness)
Peach Pit Popularity (About Friendship)

NANCY LEVENE, who shares Alex's love of softball, lives in Kansas.

Available at your local Christian bookstore.

The Pet That Never Was

"What are you bringing to show and tell, T.J.?"

His mom is coming up the stairs, his best friend, Zack, is stuck in a tree just outside the window of his third-story bedroom, and the rest of the guys are waiting at the front door to see an eight-foot pet boa constrictor that T.J. doesn't have and never did. How could one innocent question land T.J. in so much trouble?

Timothy John Fairbanks, Jr., is your typical kid next door. Through the adventures in which he and his best friend, Zack, continually find themselves, T.J. learns what it means to rely on God. With the help of his parents, he discovers how God can help him deal with even the worst of problems.

Nancy Simpson Levene, like T.J., loves sports— both soccer and softball. She is the author of the Alex series and lives in Kansas.

Chariot Books™
David C. Cook Publishing Co.